The Author

Stephanie Dagg lives in Innishannon, County Cork.

She is a mother of two children, Benjamin and Caitlín, and has been writing stories ever since she was a child. Originally from Suffolk in England, she moved to Cork in 1992.

Contents

Chapter 1
Cackling Carol's old home

Cackling Carol was a witch. She lived in a dank, gloomy cavern somewhere or other. She had lived there for hundreds of years, unnoticed by generations of local people, until the day she was spotted by Mrs Violet Dodds, Lady Mayor of the nearby town.

Cackling Carol was in the woods picking poisonous toadstools for her breakfast. She had a bad cold so she wasn't as alert as usual. Normally she would have heard Mrs Dodds approaching.

Mrs Dodds was in the woods because she was a very fat lady – and getting fatter. So she had resolved to walk in the woods every morning before going home to a light breakfast of porridge, eggs, bacon and beans.

This of course would be followed by some toast and marmalade.

Today was the first day of Mrs Dodds' fitness campaign. She had walked about a half a mile and she was breathless and tired. As she looked around for something dry and not too dirty to sit on, she spotted a hunched figure in the distance. It was Cackling Carol.

Mrs Dodds crept closer. She was horrified to see how dirty, tatty and haggard Cackling Carol looked. Now, Cackling Carol was actually quite smart and good-looking as witches go, but to our eyes she was pretty ugly and scruffy.

'Poor woman!' sighed Mrs Dodds. 'I must help her!' Mrs Dodds liked to do good deeds. She had been a very enthusiastic Girl Guide years ago and she was now a very enthusiastic Lady Mayor.

Just then, Cackling Carol got up stiffly and tottered back towards her secret cavern.

De-witched

She picked a few poisonous berries on her way and munched them, never noticing Mrs Dodds waddling and panting along behind her at a discreet distance.

That's how Mrs Dodds found out where Cackling Carol lived. And when she saw that this poor old lady lived in squalor in a cave – well, she wobbled home as quickly as she could and phoned the local welfare office.

That afternoon, as Cackling Carol was mixing up a stew of worms and mouldy sticks for tea, she had visitors. Big Roddy, her dog, suddenly sat up and growled. (Carol didn't like cats and so, a few years ago, she had got Big Roddy from a dog's home – but that's another story!) Cackling Carol looked up from her cauldron and saw some men in grey suits and a woman with a clipboard. They were all smiling at her.

Cackling Carol was so surprised that it didn't even occur to her to turn them into frogs or beetles or some other sort of creepy-crawly.

'Hello, dear,' smiled the woman. 'We've come to look after you. We'll find you a nice warm flat to live in. You can't stay in this damp old cave, it's not good for you!'

Cackling Carol's jaw dropped. She couldn't believe what was going on. This was her home, and had been since 1699 or thereabouts. She liked it.

She opened her mouth to protest but, because of her bad cold, only croaks and wheezes came out. Before she knew it, two of the men in grey suits were holding her firmly but gently by her plump arms and leading her away.

'But all my things!' she managed to squeak at last.

'Don't worry, my love. We'll bring them along for you later. I'll just make a list of what there is.' The woman glanced around and a look of horror and dismay crossed her face.

She saw the filthy cauldron full of black, bubbling stew, the battered old broom and Cackling Carol's other tatty possessions, mainly mildewed books and cracked bottles full of ghastly looking liquids.

'My dog!' wheezed Cackling Carol in horror.

Big Roddy had hidden behind Broom in the corner of the cavern.

'Oh! Have you got a dog? I'm afraid you're not allowed to have pets in the lovely sheltered housing we've got lined up for you. We'll find another home for him, dear,' smiled the woman. 'Here boy! Nice doggy!' she called.

Big Roddy poked his head out. Now he was a clever dog and he knew that he did not want these nice people getting their hands on him. So, with a despairing look at Cackling Carol, he shot off into the woods.

'Oh dear!' said the woman happily. 'Looks like he's gone for good. Never mind, dear, we'll get you a nice goldfish instead. You're allowed to have goldfish in the flats.'

With that they frog-marched Cackling Carol out to the waiting car. While their backs were turned, Broom flew off after Big Roddy.

Chapter 2
Cackling Carol's new home

It was quite late that night when, bathed and dressed in a tweed suit (courtesy of Mrs Dodds), Cackling Carol was taken to what was to be her new home. She had also been examined by a doctor who had told her that she must take better care of herself. She had also been interviewed by several important welfare officers. But since Cackling Carol could hardly talk, it had been rather a waste of time. She had just about managed to tell them her name and lie about her age and occupation. She was happy to let them assess her as a dotty old woman.

'Here we are, Carol,' said Jill Fuddleton, Cackling Carol's social worker since about an hour ago. 'Here's your own lovely flat.

You'll soon feel at home in it. I'll show you round and then leave you to get a good night's sleep. What an exciting day you've had!'

The flat was disgustingly clean and bright and airy. Cackling Carol looked in vain for a speck of dust or a cobweb. It would take years before she'd be able to get this place just as she wanted. After three hundred years, her cavern was only now just dusty enough for her liking. Her cavern! Cackling Carol sighed a deep sigh. How she missed home.

Jill thought she was sighing in delight at the flat. She beamed approvingly at Cackling Carol, said goodnight and left.

Cackling Carol wandered sadly around the flat again. It was horrible – all neat and tidy. She felt very lonely too. But just then, she heard the deepest, rumbliest woof you could ever imagine. It was Big Roddy. He had tracked Cackling Carol down at last. Cackling Carol rushed to the window and looked down. She was several floors up. There, in the flowerbed below, was Big Roddy with a big, dead rat hanging from his mouth for their supper.

Cackling Carol grinned at Big Roddy, pointed her finger at him and croaked, very croakily, a few strange words. The next instant Big Roddy was beside her, licking her hands. His tail was wagging so fast that Carol thought it was about to come off! She bent down to stroke the dog's ears.

Suddenly there was a loud thud at the window that cracked the glass. Cackling Carol jumped in alarm, then cackled in delight as she saw Broom outside. She opened the window and Broom flew gracefully in, beetles and spiders dropping onto the floor from his bristles. Cackling Carol was starting to feel a lot better.

Big Roddy sat down on the rug as if to say 'Let's have supper and go home.'

Broom agreed with him. 'Do let's go home,' he begged.

'No, no, my dears,' wheezed Cackling Carol. 'We can't go back home, not now. These people know where we live. They'd just come and get us again. We can't ever go back.' She sighed again. But she knew it was no good feeling sorry for herself. Goodness, whoever heard of a whingeing witch. Witches just got on with things. Cackling Carol would have to get on with her new life.

'No, we'll stay here for now – just long enough for my cold to go,' she told them. 'The cavern *was* a bit chilly and draughty, you know. And anyway, I can't do much magic until I get my books and bottles of spells back.'

Big Roddy shrugged. He didn't like this

bare little box that was their new home but he was happy to do whatever Cackling Carol wanted. He was a very faithful dog. And Broom was equally loyal.

'Yes, you're right,' he sighed. 'We'll stay just for a while then.' And with that he flew into a squeaky clean corner and leaned himself gingerly against the gleaming wall for a nap.

'Now,' cackled Cackling Carol. 'Where's that dead rat, Big Roddy? I'm starving.'

Chapter 3
Cackling Carol's first morning

Cackling Carol awoke next day to find the sun streaming through the curtains. It was horrid. Cackling Carol's old home had been lovely and gloomy all year round. Big Roddy obviously felt the same way because when he opened his eyes he gave a great howl of pain and dived into the nearest cupboard. It took Cackling Carol ages to coax him out, partly because Big Roddy had got stuck. He was a very big dog and the cupboard was fairly small. Broom just shuffled along the wall into the darkest corner he could find.

Just then there was a gentle knock on the door. Cackling Carol quickly stuffed the surprised Big Roddy back into the cupboard.

She opened the door a little and peeped out. There was Jill carrying a great big tray of food.

Cackling Carol sighed. Would these people never leave her alone? Jill breezed in, all smiles and niceness.

'Here we are! Breakfast! We always give new people breakfast their first day. Tuck in. I'll be back later.' She plonked the tray down on the table and was gone before Cackling Carol could croak a reply.

Big Roddy hastily squeezed out of the cupboard and rested his slobbering jaws on Cackling Carol's lap. Cackling Carol peered cautiously at the tray's contents – eggs, bacon, hot crispy bread, a jug of white stuff and a silver pot of hot brown stuff. What a peculiar meal!

Big Roddy was less fussy. He helped himself to the bacon. Cackling Carol prodded the eggs with a fork and took a slurp of the hot brown stuff from the spout of the pot. It scalded her mouth but Cackling Carol didn't even notice. Witches love really hot things. What Cackling Carol did mind was the ghastly taste. She spat the tea out in disgust. How she longed for a cup of muddy ditch water!

'Help yourself, Big Roddy," she wheezed, emptying the pot of tea over the floor. Big Roddy lapped happily away at it. He even licked up all the tea leaves.

'This will never do!' croaked Cackling Carol. 'As soon as I'm a bit better, we'll be off. But I do need my spells back.'

But Cackling Carol didn't get her spells back. Later that morning a burly man in blue overalls knocked at her door and asked for Carol W. Itch. (That was the best name Cackling Carol could think of to give the nosy social workers.) He then staggered in, carrying three full cardboard boxes.

Cackling Carol could hear her spell bottles clinking together. She rubbed her hands together in glee – now for some fun! She'd conjure up a few nasty surprises for Jill and her interfering friends!

Big Roddy and Broom were excited too and jostled each other in their rush to open the boxes. Using her long fingernails, Cackling Carol slit open the tape holding the first box shut, ripped up the flaps – and screamed! The bottles were clean and shining – and empty! Cackling Carol screamed again and Big Roddy shot back to his cupboard. Broom leapt back in alarm, crashing into the table and knocking all the breakfast things to the floor. What a racket!

There was the sound of hurrying footsteps and the door burst open. There stood Jill.

'Whatever is it, Carol?' she panted. 'Whatever was all that noise!'

Cackling Carol shot Jill a look of hatred.

'My bottles!' she hissed. 'My beautiful bottles! You've ruined them! You've cleaned them! You've – washed – them – up!"

Suddenly it was all too much. Cackling Carol crumpled to the floor in a moaning heap, to Jill's amazement – and to Big Roddy's and Broom's absolute horror. Witches aren't ones for moaning and they had never, ever seen – or rather, as they were both hiding, heard – their mistress like this. It was horrible.

Jill helped Cackling Carol up and called to someone passing by to bring a nice hot cup of tea. Cackling Carol was too weak to resist and a few moments later she found herself being forced to sip the ghastly brown stuff again while Jill patted her knee and said 'There, there,' an awful lot.

Then Jill explained that they were really only trying to help Cackling Carol. Those nasty dirty bottles had needed a cleaning. Poor Mrs Blewitt, the cleaning lady, had spent all yesterday afternoon washing them.

And it was a good job she'd done them yesterday, Jill added, because she was ill today. Apparently she was covered in warts this morning and had lost her voice. Her husband said she could only croak like a frog.

A flicker of a smile crossed Cackling Carol's face. She'd always been proud of her warts spell – it was one she'd concocted herself. She supposed the croaking was the result of a combination of several of the other spells. That would teach Mrs Blewitt a lesson!

Jill stood up to leave.

'Oh, one more surprise for you!' she said cheerily. Cackling Carol's heart sank. Not another cup of tea surely!

'Mr Parsons, our accountant, will call round soon. You never claimed your old age pension, did you dear? Apparently you've got ten years' pension money owing to you.

That's a lot of money, so Mr Parsons will help you decide what to do with it – you know, open a bank account or whatever. Anyway, I must dash,' she trilled, and zoomed off to do her next good deed.

'Well, well,' thought Cackling Carol, brightening up a bit. 'So I'm going to be rich!'

Chapter 4
Cackling Carol's new friend

And she *was* rich. Cackling Carol had never had money before. She'd never needed it in her old cavern and her old life. But now she had lots.

Despite Mr Parson's advice, Cackling Carol had taken all her money at once. She spent the rest of the day hiding it around the flat. Big Roddy got bored and slunk off to chase some rabbits in the nearby woods. Broom was happy just to snooze.

'I'll go shopping tomorrow,' muttered Cackling Carol. 'My cold is getting better and I must get things to make new spells.'

Cackling Carol would have to live in this flat until she remade her many spells. Of course she needed her books as well.

No doubt they were being scrubbed by some kind person. Cackling Carol pulled a face at the thought. Still, no need to worry – her books were as tough as old boots and a bit of cleanliness wouldn't hurt them.

Cackling Carol settled down on the floor in a corner to make a shopping list. She had only got as far as 'mice, frogs, dogfood . . .' when there was a knock at the door.

'Oh no, not again!' moaned Cackling Carol. But she got up to answer the door anyway, just in case it was someone bringing her books back.

It wasn't – it was a skinny, shifty-looking old lady. She turned on a bright smile as Cackling Carol opened the door.

'Ugh!' thought Cackling Carol. 'Why is everyone so cheerful in this place?'

She screwed her own face into a rather ghastly grin in return.

'Hello, I'm Flo Watson,' said the lady.

She stuck out a bony hand with bright red fingernails. Cackling Carol shook it gingerly.

'I heard you'd moved in and I wondered if you wanted to go to the cinema tonight.'

'Cinema?' echoed Cackling Carol. What on earth was that?

'Oh, you're teasing me!' giggled Flo. 'You're pretending you don't know what it is! I'll come round at 7 o'clock and we can go together. See you in about an hour then, dear!' And Flo was gone.

'Well, what was all that about, I wonder?' Cackling Carol asked Broom.

'Absolutely no idea!' he shrugged.

Still, Carol decided she might as well go out with Flo. She couldn't get changed since she only had Mrs Dodds' tweed suit to wear so she just added 'clothes' to her shopping list and waited for Flo to come back.

When she did, Cackling Carol beckoned her inside.

'Now, what exactly *is* this cinema and what do I need for it?'

Flo looked horrified. 'You really don't know what the cinema is? My, my! Where have you been all these years?'

Cackling Carol opened her mouth to tell her, but Flo babbled on. 'Well, it's like the telly, only bigger.' Cackling Carol was none the wiser. 'And you just need some money to pay for your ticket and of course some popcorn.'

'Oh, I've got plenty of money!' said Cackling Carol happily, and opened one of the cupboards. Piles of notes fell onto the floor. Flo's eyes nearly did too!

'Gosh!' she said weakly. Then she looked sly. Here was a friend to cherish!

'I wouldn't take all that tonight,' she advised. 'Just a bundle or two.'

Cackling Carol grabbed some money and pushed the rest back in the cupboard.

'I know,' said Flo. 'Why don't we get a taxi rather than walk to the cinema. You'd get some change then.' And with that she firmly linked her arm to Cackling Carol's and set off.

Cackling Carol had a wonderful time. The taxi was great. It was the second time she had been in one of these car things. The first time was when she had been taken away from her cavern and had been too shocked to take much notice. This time she really enjoyed the comfortable, warm ride. It was nice!

It was better than being stuck on an open-air broom. Perhaps she could get herself a nice car. Big Roddy might like it. And it would give Broom a rest.

And as for the cinema, well, it was fun. The darkness reminded Cackling Carol of her gloomy cavern so she felt quite at home. She wasn't that bothered about the film which seemed to be very complicated.

Cackling Carol and Flo shared some popcorn – well, Flo ate all the popcorn and Cackling Carol ate the cardboard carton which she thought was absolutely delicious. Flo didn't want to upset her new, rich friend so she didn't say anything about this strange behaviour. Flo also ate several ice-creams and at least ten chocolate bars which Cackling Carol bought for her.

Cackling Carol and Flo got another taxi home. As they got out, Cackling Carol mentioned that she needed to go shopping the next day. Flo at once offered to go with her. Then they went to their flats, very pleased with each other.

Chapter 5
Cackling Carol's new life

Cackling Carol couldn't wait to go shopping. She got up while it was still dark, put on the horrid suit, filled a plastic bag with money and sat and waited for Flo. Big Roddy and Broom came and sat with her for some company, but Cackling Carol impatiently pushed them away.

'Not now,' she snapped. 'I'm off shopping soon.'

Broom dawdled back to his corner and Big Roddy glared balefully at Cackling Carol before walking off in a huff and jumping on the bed. He and Broom were both getting very bored in the flat.

A little later, Flo arrived. She was in a flap.

'Oh, Carol, dear! I can't come after all. I've lost my purse! All my money was in it!'

She started to sob. Big Roddy, peeping out of the bedroom, noticed there were no tears.

'Oh, have some of my money!' offered Cackling Carol. 'I've got plenty. Please come shopping. There are so many things I need.'

'Well, if you insist!' smiled Flo, the tragedy of the missing purse forgotten at once. 'Off we go then.'

Cackling Carol didn't even look back at Broom and Big Roddy as she left.

Shopping was even better than the cinema. Cackling Carol found she had enough money to buy all the things she and Flo wanted – and Flo seemed to want an awful lot.

Cackling Carol forgot all about buying things to make spells. Under Flo's influence she got some nice clothes that the assistant said were very 'fashionable'. Cackling Carol kept one of her new outfits on and dumped the hated tweed suit in a bin.

Then Flo talked Cackling Carol into getting her hair cut short and her fingernails manicured. The manicurist was rather green in the face after she'd cleaned Cackling Carol's fingernails.

Finally, at a supermarket, Cackling Carol bought a trolleyful of vegetables. She still didn't trust all this modern food.

Flo asked for a lot of very expensive things but Cackling Carol didn't mind. She forgot about getting Big Roddy any food.

Cackling Carol was exhausted when she got back to the flat. She put down her heavy shopping and unlocked the door. She went in. Big Roddy came bounding towards her but suddenly stopped dead in his tracks! This wasn't his mistress! This was a stranger with a bobbed hair cut and a trouser suit. He ran and hid in his cupboard!

It took Cackling Carol ages to persuade Big Roddy that she *was* Cackling Carol. Big Roddy recoiled from the clean fingers that reached in to stroke him. He refused to lay his head on the trouser-suited legs at supper time. He sulked all night.

Broom was pretty horrified as well. However, Cackling Carol didn't even notice. Tired as she was, she went to the cinema again with Flo after quickly changing into another new outfit.

And that became the pattern of Cackling Carol's days. She would go shopping with Flo during the day and out to the cinema at night. There were a few other things to do too, like go to the dentist to have some false teeth fitted and the opticians for some new reading glasses. Cackling Carol's piles of money grew rapidly smaller.

Her spell books arrived but she never got round to looking at them. Big Roddy spent

more and more time in his cupboard and
Broom hardly moved for days on end.
Cackling Carol had more or less forgotten
about them. She never even mentioned the
subject of leaving the flat. So, one day, while
she was out, Broom and Big Roddy left
together to find a new home on their own.

Chapter 6
Cackling Carol's old friends

It was several days before Cackling Carol realised that Broom and Big Roddy had gone. She'd been particularly busy for a day or two and was out very late several nights running. It was only when she decided to have a lazy morning at home that she noticed she was alone. She was putting on some face powder (Flo had advised her to get some make-up) when she sneezed and dropped the powder compact.

'Bother!' said Cackling Carol. Under Flo's influence she had become quite tidy and house-proud. 'Broom, sweep the mess up!' No Broom appeared.

'Broom!' she called again.

Still nothing.

'Big Roddy, come and clean the floor with your tail!' she pleaded.

Big Roddy didn't appear either.

Now that was odd. Cackling Carol hadn't seen either of them go out that morning. In fact, she hadn't seen them at all that morning. Or, come to think of it, yesterday morning either.

43

Suddenly Cackling Carol was in a panic. Had that social worker, Jill Fuddleton, come round one day and found them? Or had they left of their own accord? No, surely not – not her faithful dog and Broom.

Cackling Carol searched every corner of the flat. She checked all the cupboards. No Big Roddy. No Broom. Cackling Carol sat down on the bed. She looked at the gleaming spell bottles, still in their boxes. She looked at the pile of neglected spell books. She looked at the clothes in the wardrobe and at the jewellery and the make-up on the dressing table. She looked at the little bit of money left in her new leather handbag.

What had happened to her?

She'd been de-witched, that's what! Bother these interfering do-gooders! Look what they'd done to her. Look what they'd turned her into – a flat-dwelling, cinema-going, made-up and dressed-up shopaholic!

No wonder Big Roddy and Broom had left.

Something wet and warm splashed onto Cackling Carol's hands which were resting on her lap. It was a tear. Cackling Carol hadn't cried for over two hundred and fifty years, not since her Auntie Nellie had flown off one night in a storm never to be seen again. Cackling Carol had loved Auntie Nellie (although witches rarely admit to loving anything, except mischief). And Cackling Carol loved Big Roddy and Broom.

They were her real friends. Flo was only a pretend friend. Cackling Carol could see that now. Flo only liked Cackling Carol's money, not Cackling Carol.

She clenched her fists and got up. She rubbed off all the make-up. She took off the jewellery. She took out her dentures. (She had to leave the trouser suit on though.) She found a suitcase and shoved as many of the spell bottles and books into it as she could. She emptied the money out of her handbag and into her case, but then she pulled it all out again. Grasping the notes and coins in her hand she stormed off to Flo's flat. She pounded on the door.

Flo opened it a tiny bit and peeped anxiously around the edge. 'Oh, it's you, dear, whatever—' but Cackling Carol interrupted her.

'Here!' she spat. 'Here, take the rest of my money, you scheming toad! You've had most

of it already!' She hurled the money at Flo and stomped off, leaving Flo in a flood of tears.

Cackling Carol picked up her case and walked out of the flat – for good. At the front door she passed Jill who gaped at her. Cackling Carol heard Jill calling her and heard a patter of footsteps behind her. Cackling Carol whirled round and summoned her few remaining magic powers. She screamed some strange words (which she'd almost forgotten she knew) and Jill was frozen to the spot. She wouldn't be frozen for long.

However, with any luck, it would be long enough for Cackling Carol to get away.

Cackling Carol hurried along the streets until she reached the edge of town. Then she stopped for a moment.

'Big Roddy! Broom!' she called. 'I'm coming! I don't care how long it takes, but I'll find you! I'll never let those do-gooders get their hands on me again.'

And did she find them? You'll have to wait and see . . .